Bea Garcia

TALE
of a
SCAREDY
DOG

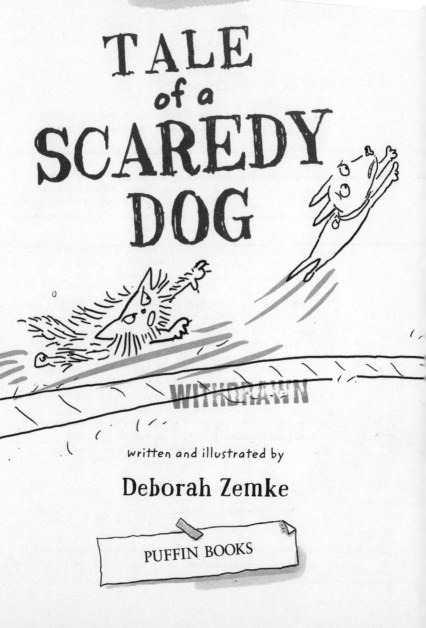

written and illustrated by

Deborah Zemke

PUFFIN BOOKS

PUFFIN BOOKS
An imprint of Penguin Random House LLC
375 Hudson Street
New York, New York 10014

First published in the United States of America by Dial Books for Young Readers, 2018.
Published by Puffin Books, an imprint of Penguin Random House LLC, 2018

Text and illustrations copyright © 2018 by Deborah Zemke

THE LIBRARY OF CONGRESS HAS CATALOGED THE DIAL BOOKS FOR YOUNG READERS
EDITION AS FOLLOWS:
Names: Zemke, Deborah, author, illustrator.
Title: Tale of a scaredy-dog / Deborah Zemke.
Description: New York, NY : Dial Books for Young Readers, [2018] | Series:
Bea Garcia ; 3 | Summary: "Bea Garcia loves art, especially when she gets
to draw pictures of her dog, Sophie. When Sophie runs away after an
encounter with the neighbor's cat, Bea has to find a way to
bring her home again."—Provided by publisher.
Identifiers: LCCN 2017045648| ISBN 9780735229389 (hardback) | ISBN
9780735229396 (paperback) | ISBN 9780735229402 (ebook)
Subjects: | CYAC: Dogs—Fiction. | Lost and found possessions—Fiction. |
Neighbors—Fiction. | Drawing—Fiction. | Hispanic Americans—Fiction. |
BISAC: JUVENILE FICTION / Readers / Chapter Books. | JUVENILE FICTION /
Social Issues / Friendship. | JUVENILE FICTION / School & Education.
Classification: LCC PZ7.Z423 Tal 2018 | DDC [Fic]—dc23 LC record available at
https://lccn.loc.gov/2017045648

Puffin Books ISBN 9780735229396

Printed in the United States of America
1 3 5 7 9 10 8 6 4 2

For all the kids who commit acts of
bravery every day

Chapter 1
SOPHIE'S ILLUSTRATED DICTIONARY OF DOG

Author, noun: someone who writes a book, article, or anything

Here's the author of *Sophie's Illustrated Dictionary of Dog*. Yep—a dog. Not just any dog, though. It's my Sophie, the smartest dog in the world.

Here she is holding a pencil. Sophie loves pencils. She doesn't love to write with them because paws are not very good for holding pencils. My new almost best friend Judith Einstein told me why.

That's a fancy way of saying that paws are not very good for holding pencils. Sophie does love to chew pencils, especially the outer wood part.

The gray inside writing part makes her sick.

I love pencils, too, only I don't usually chew them. I usually draw with them.

This is me, Bea Garcia.

I draw pictures of EVERYTHING. Here's Sophie chasing a stick in our backyard.

Here's Super Sophie chasing a stick in outer space.

I write words with pencils, too. I'm writing the words and drawing the pictures for this book, the one you're holding in your hands.

I'm also writing the words that Sophie tells me for her dictionary.

You're transcribing Sophie's book.

That's a fancy way of saying I'm writing the words that Sophie tells me.

Human, noun: a dog's best friend

JUST KIDDING! Sophie doesn't really speak English—or Spanish—or any other human language.

She does understand some human words.

Other words she only understands when she wants to.

Sophie speaks Dog.

Woof means everything—*yes, no, up, down, why, here, there, no way*. It all depends on how she says it.

When Sophie calls me Woof she means it as a compliment.

I'm Sophie's human. She has other humans, like my little brother, the Big Pest, but I'm the only one who understands EVERYTHING she says.

Sophie doesn't just say *Woof*. She talks
with her tail, too.

See? Here she's saying . . .

I learned Sophie's special tail language
by drawing her.

Right now Sophie's saying . . .

Here's why. This is Bert.

He's a monster. Really.

He scares my little brother and my not-so-brave-but-really-smart dog, Sophie.

Bert lives next door in the house where my best friend, Yvonne, lived until she moved a million miles away to Australia.

Bert doesn't scare me. He makes me mad. He calls me names.

Lately he's been calling me . . .

Einstein tried to make me feel better.

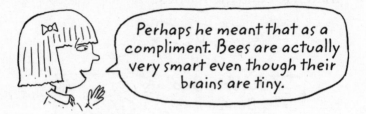

Perhaps he meant that as a compliment. Bees are actually very smart even though their brains are tiny.

But compliments are nice and Bert is not. Getting a compliment from Bert would be like eating ice cream made out of onions. Even if you put a cherry on top, it would taste awful.

Einstein and I sit next to each other in class. She knows everything. Well, almost everything. She doesn't know monsters.

But Bert is very real.

That's my mom.

I'm not sure my mom understands monsters, either.

You can be nice and stand up for yourself at the same time.

That's true if you had superpowers, like Super Sophie, the world's smartest AND bravest dog.

Drawing is like a superpower because you can draw EVERYTHING. You can draw what really happens, and you can draw what you WISH would happen.

See? Here's Sophie standing up to Bert and being nice, too.

*In Dog that means *Please go away*.

Here's Sophie really. Paws may not be good for holding pencils, but they're great for running away from scary stuff.

Here's Sophie at the top of the crab-apple tree in our backyard. She runs fast, fast enough to get away from Bert. But now she's too scared to come down.

Chapter 2

SOPHIE'S SECRET

Biscuit, noun: a cookie for dogs often shaped like a bone

Sophie loves biscuits more than anything except peanut butter cookies.

That's why Sophie isn't scared of Fireman Dave even though he's riding a big noisy fire truck. Fireman Dave smells like biscuits.

Einstein says . . .

That means they can smell a million times more than we can.

I'm not sure how that works, but I know that when Sophie smells biscuits she smells love.

Here we all are, her family, giving her biscuits and love. Me, my mom and dad, and my little brother, the Big Pest.

But really, we're her second family.

Here's her first family, her dog family. Left to right are her mother, father, brother, and sisters.

Bruiser
Crunch
Growl
Slobber
Snap
Weasel

As you can see, they were a pretty terrifying pack, especially if you are the smallest and named Weasel.

So now you know Sophie's secret. She was the runt of the litter, which means that not only was she the smallest, she was the way smallest, the puniest pup in the pack. That's why she got the name Weasel.

I was the littlest in our family, too, when I picked her to be my puppy. That was before the Big Pest was born.

I didn't pick her because she was the smallest but because she came right to me and said . . .

I understood right away that she was saying . . .

See how her tail is down and scared?

On the way home we thought of new names for my new puppy.

Nothing seemed right until . . .

*That means YES! in Dog.

Sophie grew up and isn't puny any-more. She's not huge, either. She's just the right size to curl up beside me in bed.

She still gets scared of things like trucks and vacuum cleaners.

And Bert. Of course with Bert she has good reason to be scared. He doesn't smell like biscuits. He smells like onions.

Chapter 3
WORSE THAN HOMEWORK

Chew, verb: to bite, munch, chomp, crunch, gnaw, and nibble

I'm not afraid of Bert, but there's no way I'm going to his house.

I went there a million times when it was Yvonne's house but not once since Bert moved in.

I've never been invited, and I wouldn't go even if I was. Not even if Bert asked nicely which he didn't and wouldn't and couldn't. His house probably smells like onions.

Here are Sophie and me on our way to Bert's house. It wasn't my idea. It was my teacher's, Mrs. Grogan. She said it was homework.

But homework is work you do at home, and this is work I have to do at Bert's house.

Here's Bert on his way to my house.

Here's why we had to go to each other's houses. In class our assignment was to interview another student about their life.

It would have been fun if I could have interviewed anybody except him. Even Walter the bunny would have been better.

I begged Mrs. Grogan to let me interview Einstein instead of Bert.

But Mrs. Grogan didn't budge. So here's my interview of Bert:

Meet Bert the monster
By Bea Garcia
Family GRRRRRRRR!
Pets GRRRRRRRR!
Hobbies GRRRRRRRR!
Favorite food GRRRRRRRR!
Favorite book GRRRRRRRR!
What you would never guess about me GRRRRRRRRRRR!
Place of birth GRRRRRR!

All of which is untrue. I know for a fact that Bert has a mother. She even looks like him if he was tall and pretty and his hair was combed and he didn't scrunch up his face like a monster and call me names.

Here's Bert's interview of me:

Bert scribbled things I didn't say. But even if I hadn't crumpled up the paper you still wouldn't have been able to read it because his writing is so bad. You can imagine what Mrs. Grogan thought about our interviews.

Bea, Bert, I know you can do better than this.

It's not fair! Can you imagine what my little brother might say about me? Bert doesn't have a little brother, at least not one that I've seen.

When I got home I made my mom promise not to let the Big Pest answer any questions.

Then I made sure the Big Pest couldn't talk.

Just kidding. I didn't really put a Band-Aid over my little brother's mouth.

But I did give my mom this list of correct answers.

Meet **Beatrice Holmes Garcia**

By **Bert the Monster**

Family **Mom, Dad, the Big Pest, mis abuelos, which is Spanish for grandparents**

Pets **Sophie, the smartest dog in the world**

Hobbies **Artist and Lion Tamer**

Favorite food **peanut butter cookies**

Favorite book **My Life in Pictures**

What you would never guess about me

I can fly around the world!

Place of birth **California, as in HOLLYWOOD!**

And I made her promise not to let Bert into my room. Bert has been on my front porch and in the crabapple tree in my backyard. But he has never been inside my actual house.

Mi casa NO *es tu casa*, Bert, which in Spanish is like saying STAY OUT!

Chapter 4
INTO THE MONSTER'S LAIR

Lair, noun: a wild animal's
resting place

I'm not scared of going to Bert's house because I'm not scared of Bert. Einstein says monsters are imaginary, so that means Bert is imaginary, too.

Besides it's really Yvonne's old house. It's just the same except now there's a fence all the way around the backyard. And there aren't any flowers on the porch, and the front door is painted yucky green instead of bright red.

There isn't really a *Beware of Monster* sign in his front yard, but there should be.

I used to look out my bedroom window and see Yvonne's window. We waved good night to each other every night.

Now the curtains to her bedroom are closed, which is good because it would give me nightmares to see Bert's face the last thing before I went to sleep.

I'm taking Sophie with me to Bert's house.

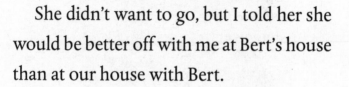

She didn't want to go, but I told her she would be better off with me at Bert's house than at our house with Bert.

*In dog that means *Do you promise?*
I didn't tell Sophie what Einstein told me.

Cookies may not be healthy, but they can be helpful. Here we are, walking past Bert on the sidewalk between our houses.

See how Bert just disappeared?

We walked up to the porch and rang the bell.

Here we are eating cookies in Bert's kitchen.

It doesn't look like a monster's kitchen, does it? A monster wouldn't have pretty curtains. Bert's mother is as nice as Bert is awful. She answered the first question without me even asking.

Sophie thought I should tell Bert's mom the truth—that Bert and I aren't friends. Sophie even wanted me to tell her that we used our superpowers to make Bert imaginary. Instead I asked the second question:

Does Bert have a hobby?

Yes, come upstairs and I'll show you.

Prepare yourself for the next picture.

Welcome to Bert's laboratory. His hobby is cryptozoology.

Cryptowho?

It means he loves monsters.

This really is Bert's room. I know it's so dark you can't see much, but that's probably a good thing. Be glad that I can't draw smells because it smells worse than onions. Bert's hobby, whatever it was, was making me gag. You can imagine how Sophie felt with her super-sniffer nose.

Bert's mom must have thought it smelled bad, too, because she opened the window.

I WISH I hadn't asked.

Chapter 5

MONSTERS HAVE PETS, TOO.

Pet, noun: a tame animal kept for companionship and pleasure

GGGGGGGFFF

B ig Kitty was big, but she was definitely
NOT a kitty.

She was a monster! An orange furry
beast with glowing eyes and . . .

MONSTER paws!

Sophie didn't run. She FLEW out the window.

The orange monster flew after her . . .

and they both disappeared.

Where did they go?

Sophie came.

Big Kitty came, too, chasing Sophie.

Bert's mom and I ran downstairs and out to the backyard.

Big Kitty chased
Sophie
up and
down,
down and
up . . .

and
DOWN.

Sophie came down, flying through my arms and out the gate.

We went flying after her, but none of us could run as fast as Sophie.

She raced next door to our backyard where the world's only tree-climbing dog jumped into the crabapple tree . . .

followed by Big Kitty.

Everybody ran out to see what was happening.

Sometimes it's impossible to be nice AND stand up for yourself.

But while I was standing up for myself Sophie got down all by herself.

She skittered away as fast as she could, down our driveway to the sidewalk.

Sophie ran around Max Pettigrew's wagon and . . .

through Mrs. Ginwalla's flower garden.

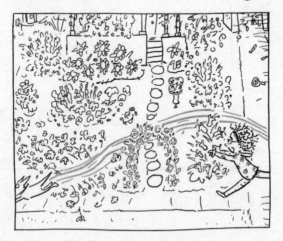

She got to the corner . . .

but didn't stop.

I stopped.

I looked for Sophie. She was gone. Out of sight.

I didn't stay. I stepped off the curb.

Then my dad took my hand. We looked both ways and crossed the street.

Chapter 6
SEARCHING FOR SOPHIE

Chase, verb: to tear after someone or something very quickly so you can catch them

Here we are walking up Greenwood Street and down Blue Meadow Drive. I wanted to run but my dad held my hand tight. We crossed Red Leaf Lane.

We trudged up Laurel Mountain Drive.

We walked and walked. My dad kept hold of my hand and told me over and over...

I wanted to believe him. But when it started to drizzle, it felt like the rain was saying LOST FOREVER.

Who was that? The only person who called me Beatrice was . . .

It started raining harder. Einstein ran into her house.

She came back with an umbrella.

It was the biggest cookie I'd ever seen.
It smelled like peanut butter—my favorite,
and Sophie's, too.

My dad and I walked up Flowers Street and over to Acorn Drive. All the way I kept thinking *maybe Sophie is home, maybe Sophie is home.* Einstein's cookie didn't smell like fish oil. It smelled like peanut butter. It smelled like home. *Maybe Sophie is home.*

Chapter 7:
¡PERDIDO!
LOST DOG!

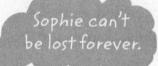

Perdido, adjective: Spanish for lost, but not forever

Sophie can't be lost forever.

But Sophie was NOT home when we got home.

Everybody else was there, including Fireman Dave. It had stopped raining. Big Kitty was still stuck in the tree.

That meow wasn't Big Kitty. It was Bert. Now you know what it sounds like when a monster cries. Just as awful as when they growl. I almost felt sorry for him. Almost.

Big Kitty didn't come down. Fireman
Dave held out a treat.

I don't know how something that
smelled like rotten fish could be called a
treat. Big Kitty thought it smelled . . .

She jumped into Fireman Dave's arms.
Big Kitty rode down like she was a hero.

Everybody crowded around Big Kitty and fed her stinky fish treats. How could they all be so happy? It was Bert's cat who chased Sophie, and now Big Kitty was home and Sophie was still lost.

That wasn't Big Kitty or Bert. That was me. My eyes glowed, and I stretched my monster paws toward Bert.

Bert ran home.

But that didn't make me feel any better.

It didn't bring Sophie home. She was still …

LOST FOREVER.

My dad told me he knew how worried I was about Sophie.

Don't blame Bert.

It's his fault! He's a monster, and his cat is a monster. She tried to eat Sophie! If you'd seen his room, you'd know.

His mother told me he LOVED monsters. She said he was a cryptozoologist. That means he loves monsters!

Maybe he loves his pet, too.

Maybe. I picked up Einstein's cookie and went in the house.

My parents tried to make me feel better.
Here are all the *don't worries* they told me.

Don't worry, Sophie will be home when she gets hungry.

But Sophie is always hungry.

Don't worry, she can't have gone far.

Sophie is fast, especially when she's scared.

Don't worry, Sophie will find her own way home.

How will she find her way? She can't read the street signs.

Don't worry, someone will find her and bring her home.

But how will they know where home is?

Our phone number is on her tag.

But how will they know she's lost?

Here I am, drawing a LOST DOG poster so everyone will know Sophie is lost.

Now you know why I call my little brother the Big Pest even though his real name is Pablo. He just grabs my stuff. He NEVER asks first.

No way. Nobody could be as sad as me.
Then I looked at the Big Pest and changed
my mind. I gave him a piece of paper and a
black crayon. Here's what he drew.

It didn't look like Sophie. It didn't even
look like a dog.

The Big Pest looked like he was going to cry again, so I added two ears, two Sophie eyes, and her superpower nose to his scribble.

Then I showed him how to make a friendly tail. Now it looked like Sophie after she played in the mud.

I wrote Sophie's name in cool letters at the top.

My mom wrote the rest. She has very neat handwriting.

We made four more posters. I drew a different Sophie on each one. The Big Pest helped. See the friendly tails? He drew those.

SOPHiE

LOST DOG!
¡PERDIDO!
Small, smart white dog once
known as Weasel. Has a secret
brown patch on her tummy.
Loves cookies.
Call 7

SOPHiE

LOST DOG!
¡PERDIDO!
Small, smart white dog once
known as Weasel. Has a secret
brown patch on her tummy.
Loves cookies.
Call 750-4

Sophie

LOST DOG!
¡PERDIDO!
Small, smart white dog once
known as Weasel. Has a secret
brown patch on her tummy.
Loves cookies.
Call 750-

SOPHiE

LOST DOG!
¡PERDIDO!
Small, smart white dog once
known as Weasel. Has a secret
brown patch on her tummy.
Loves cookies.
Call 750-

My mom made us wear our raincoats even though it wasn't raining anymore. Here we are putting up a poster on the corner and . . .

at the grocery store and . . .

the library and . . .

the fire station.

But Sophie wasn't home when we got home. We put the last poster on our front door.

Dinner was full of maybes.

Maybe someone will see the posters and find Sophie.

Maybe they'll take her home and then call us.

Maybe she'll find her own way home.

Maybe she's already on her way home.

But maybe a scaredy dog like Sophie would just run until she couldn't run anymore and end up lost in the middle of NOWHERE! With NO WAY HOME!

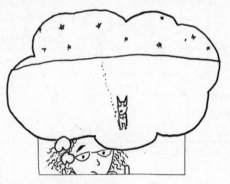

The doorbell rang.

Maybe she's at the door right now!

Sophie wasn't at the door. It was Bert and his mom with cookies.

At least the cookies didn't smell like onions. They smelled like peanut butter.

Chapter 8

NIGHTMARE ON
WOODLAWN STREET

Here I am staring at the fake stars on my ceiling and trying to pretend that Sophie was curled up beside me.

Was Sophie cold? Wet? Was she hungry? Was she scared? What if Sophie was dognapped by a pack of wolves?

The Big Pest was even more worried than I was. I tried to make him feel better.

I told him Sophie was on her way home when . . .

GGGFRRRRRRROWL!

HOME

Sophie looked up at the sky. Where was that noise coming from? The stars were blinking orange. And getting closer.

Sophie could smell...onions? No, fish! Rotten fish!!! The orange stars were Big Kitties!

Was Sophie scared?

Sophie was brave until...

Sophie closed her eyes and all 220 million of the olfactory receptors in her super sniffer nose. She used her super power to IMAGINE cookies. Peanut butter cookies that smelled like HOME.

Then she ran off like a scaredy dog so that all of the Big Kitties would chase her.

101

Here I am, dreaming Sophie home.

Chapter 9
THE GREAT COOKIE TRAIL

Cookie, noun: a delicious treat for kids and sometimes dogs, too

RINGALING!

Here I am running around the kitchen with the Big Pest! The phone was ringing! Someone found Sophie! Hooray!

The phone rang again.

Fireman Dave called and Mr. Pettigrew next door called. Neither of them had seen Sophie, but they promised to keep an eye out.

One person called to say how much they liked the poster and could they have one if we ever found Sophie.

It was a compliment that felt like

My mom tried to make me feel better.

They were Bert's mom's peanut butter cookies, the same kind that Sophie and I ate at Bert's house yesterday. They were yummy. And they smelled like

I looked at the Big Pest.

And that's when it hit me. I suddenly saw how to get Sophie home!

I almost kissed the Big Pest! But I had work to do. I grabbed the plate and ran outside.

The Big Pest followed me.

I raced to the corner and stopped. This was the last place that I saw Sophie.

I took a cookie and got down on the sidewalk.

I never should have let the Big Pest hold
the plate.

Now instead of a trail leading straight home, there were bits of cookie scattered everywhere. I looked at the Big Pest.

I held the plate myself and started again.

It took a long time but here's the Great Cookie Trail, running up the sidewalk from the corner, past Mrs. Ginwalla's flowers, past the Pettigrews', to HOME.

ALMOST. I was almost home when I
ran out of cookies.

I looked at the Big Pest. You can't see him because he's covered in crumbs.

Then I remembered Einstein's cookie just for Sophie. Thank you, Einstein! I ran into the house. When I came back out the Big Pest was gone.

Chapter 10

SOPHIE SAVES THE DAY!

Family, noun: Some animals, especially humans, live together through thick and thin even if their little brother is a Big Pest.

Bert was there with Big Kitty. On MY driveway.

What do YOU want?
I want my cookies!
This is SOPHIE'S cookie!
I want MY cookies, the ones my mom made for me and gave to you!
See those crumbs on the sidewalk? Those are YOUR cookies.

I looked at what was once a trail of crumbs. They were gone!

The crumbs were gone! Sophie must have sniffed out the trail and eaten her way home!

She was someplace nearby, I could just feel it.

Sophie didn't come.

Sophie fetched.

ALMOST. Sophie caught the cookie.
But she didn't bring it back.

Instead she ran off just like a scaredy dog, chased by Big Kitty and Bert. And me. Big Kitty could run fast.

But Sophie ran faster, back and forth on the sidewalk between Bert's house and our house.

She ran round and round . . .

up and
down . . .

until . . .

she STOPPED.

125

Sophie turned, looked Big Kitty in the eye and politely said . . .

*That means *If you wanted some of my cookie, all you had to do was ask.* But Big Kitty was too tired to ask for anything. Besides she hated peanut butter.

Unlike Bert who grabbed the cookie and took a bite.

Bert ran home with Big Kitty. Sophie's cookie was crumbled, but it didn't matter.

Sophie came home.

Just kidding. Sophie is smart but she could never say that much, at least that I could understand.

Where she spent the night is her secret. Wherever she was, it was muddy. She looked just like the picture that the Big Pest drew.

Which reminded me . . .

*Which means *Follow me.*

Here's the Big Pest stuck in the crab-apple tree. He got scared and ran there when Big Kitty and Bert showed up.

Here are Sophie and me helping him get down all by himself. And all of us woofing how happy we are.

Chapter 11
WOOF!

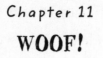

Illustrator, noun: an artist who tells stories with pictures

Here I am, painting Sophie's dog family on the fence. Notice anything different about them?

That's right! They're not scary! They're all smiling with love!

And it's really true! Because guess what? The families of Sophie's dog family all saw the posters and called to say that they hoped we found Weasel.

*That means YES, *we did!!!*

We had a painting party in the backyard and everybody came. Even Fireman
Dave without his big noisy truck. Einstein
brought a whole plate of giant peanut butter cookies—without the fish oil.

Bert and Big Kitty came, too.

Bert wanted me to add Big Kitty but I said no way. Dogs only! He can paint Big Kitty himself on his side of the fence.

There is no way I'm going back to Bert's house. Not even to jump on his trampoline, which would be fun if it wasn't Bert's.

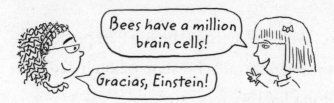

And thanks to Einstein, I know for a fact that bees are really smart so I'm just going to act like Bert gave me a compliment—one that smells like honey, not onions.

See? I'm giving Bert one of Einstein's 100 percent peanut butter cookies.

We're all artists. The Big Pest painted all the friendly tails. Einstein painted 220 million olfactory receptors.

Just kidding! But Einstein did paint Crunch's and Slobber's noses.

Sophie painted a part with her tail. It was by accident, but I think it looks good. And now her friendly tail is as blue as the sky.

It took a while but Sophie and I finished her *Dictionary of Dog* that we started at the beginning of this book. Einstein helped. Turn the page. You can read the whole thing from A to Z.

SOPHIE'S ILLUSTRATED DICTIONARY OF DOG

Arf, exclamation: No dogs say Arf. That's something that cats made up to make dogs sound silly. Cats are tricky critters, you can ask any dog. *See* Cat.

Author, noun: Someone who writes a book, article, or anything important. Sophie is the very first dog author.

Bark, noun or verb: Sophie made me put this joke in here.

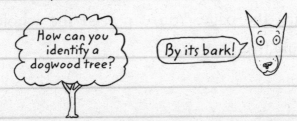

She wants everyone to know that most dogs have a sense of humor. Some dogs think it's funny to bark at two o'clock in the morning just for fun. Most humans probably don't see what's funny about that but maybe if they tried barking for no reason they'd understand.

Best Friend, noun: You've probably heard the saying that a dog is man's best friend. That's dog, not cat, not gerbil, not salamander. What I've learned is that a girl can have more than one best friend like Yvonne and Einstein and Sophie and even a little brother like the Big Pest. But not Bert. NO WAY!

Biscuit, noun: a cookie for dogs often shaped like a bone and used as a treat. This is a word that every human needs to know and should use often. Some dogs will do anything, including fetching, rolling over, playing dead, and worst of all, begging, just to hear the word biscuit, and maybe get one as a reward. Einstein says that in England people call cookies biscuits, but I'm still going to call a cookie a cookie.

Bite, verb or noun: You guess. Which of these bites is dog and which is human?

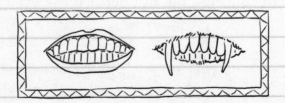

Bone, noun: Artists always draw bones like this with two straight lines and knobs on the ends. But bones don't really look like that. Biscuits do.

Bravery, noun: In Sophie's opinion, there's no shame in being sensitive. In fact, it makes sense to run away from anything that really is scary or sounds scary like vacuum cleaners or big trucks.

Cat, noun: a furry four-legged creature who thinks it's better than everyone else, including humans. Sophie says most humans think the same thing about themselves.

Chase, verb: to tear after someone or something very quickly so you can catch them. If you are a monster you eat them after you catch them. If you are a smart dog like Sophie, you chase sticks and balls and butterflies just for fun and you never eat them.

Chew, verb: to bite, munch, chomp, crunch, gnaw, or nibble. Sophie once tried to chew a tire on the car but couldn't get her jaws around it, which is a good thing because it's hard to go anywhere in a three-wheeled car. Here are some of Sophie's favorite things to chew:

my brother's sock   my dad's glasses   my book   my mom's lipstick   pencil   stick

Cookie, noun: No one has to tell you what this is! Cookies are sweet to eat and can't be beat! All dogs love cookies, and kids do, too. They are way better than biscuits. Peanut butter cookies are Sophie's favorite. Who took a bite out of her cookie?

Dog, noun: If you're reading this book you already know what a dog is. There are hundreds of different kinds of dogs, but most dogs are all mixed up like Sophie. Here's Sophie dressed up as a Dalmatian at the fire station.

Dream, noun: thoughts, feelings, or pictures that go through your mind when you're sleeping but seem as real as if you were wide awake. Most dogs dream about chasing things.

Einstein, noun: Judith Einstein is the smartest girl in the universe and my more than almost best friend. She is the trusted source for this dictionary, which means she really knows about dogs, not because she has a dog but because she's read all the books there are to read about dogs. Everything she says is . . .

ACCURATE

That means it's 100% CORRECT.

Family, noun: Some animals, especially humans, live together even if their little brother is a Big Pest.

Garbage disposal, noun: a machine usually found in the kitchen which gets rid of stuff no one can eat. Dogs can be excellent and efficient garbage disposals. If your dinner includes spinach, just place your dog right under the table. Dogs will clean up that spinach in no time, though it's best if you give them some of your meat loaf to help wash it down.

Growl, verb: to make a dark low sound in order to terrify others, even and especially when the critter growling is terrified itself. While it's true that some dogs growl, Sophie does not, and says that growling is more typical of wild animals, warthogs, and monsters like Bert.

Home, noun: the place where your heart is.

Illustrator, noun: An artist who tells stories with pictures. I, Bea Garcia, am the official illustrator of this dictionary and of this book.

Lair, noun: a wild animal's resting place. Smart animals like dogs prefer to sleep in soft beds with pillows.

Paws, noun: Paws are like running shoes. But paw prints aren't one of a kind like fingerprints. Nose prints are! Isn't that weird? Guess who told me that? *See* Einstein.

Perdido, adjective: Spanish for lost.

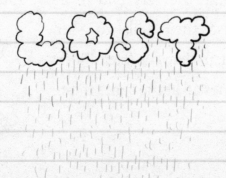

Pet, noun: a tame animal kept by humans for companionship and pleasure. Dogs almost always make the best pets unless you are a monster, in which case a cat like Big Kitty is perfect.

Smell, verb: Dogs can smell a million times more than humans. There are some smells, though, like rotten fish, that I, as a human, would rather NOT smell.

Tail, noun: the very end of most animals. Dogs use their tails to show enthusiasm, fear, or friendliness, sometimes all at the same time.

Tree, noun: a woody plant that grows from the earth to the sky. Trees are excellent places for cats to get stuck in and for best friends to dream in.

Woof: That's Sophie saying, Thanks for reading my dictionary!

**Don't miss Bea Garcia's
exciting beginning in
My Life in Pictures!**

What would Bea Garcia do
with a magic pencil?

Find out in

The Curse of Einstein's Pencil!

Here I am, at the top of a giant tree named Emily.

You're probably wondering why anyone would name a tree.

I'm wondering why anyone would want to cut her down.

I have to stop them! But how?

Find out in Book 4 about Bea Garcia, Artist

A Tree Named Emily

Coming in 2019